T
GREATEST
TREASURE
OF ALL

Narinder Dhami

Illustrated by **Teresa Martinez**

OXFORD
UNIVERSITY PRESS

Letter from the Author

I always enjoy writing stories set in India because my dad was Indian, and I've visited the country many times since I was a little girl. It's an amazing place where colours seem brighter and stronger than they ever have before!

There's so much to see: famous monuments like the Taj Mahal, ancient temples, wonderful wildlife – including tigers, elephants and monkeys – and miles and miles of long sandy beaches. Goa, where my story is set, is a very popular holiday destination for tourists from all over the world, as well as for Indian people themselves from big, bustling cities like Mumbai, Delhi and Kolkata. That's what I love about India – it's such a world of contrasts.

I've been a writer for quite a few years now and it's still my dream job. I get to sit around all day making up stories in my head. How great is that? I really hope you enjoy this one!

Narinder Dhami

Chapter 1
Gran's Surprise

'Get off me!' Vikram was trying to push his twin sister Anita off the sofa with one hand, while holding the TV remote control high above his head in the other. No way was Anita getting hold of it. 'I'm watching *Indian Superheroes Save the World*!'

'But I want to watch *Katie Patel, Girl Detective* on the other channel!' Anita emphasized her words by whacking her brother over the head with a cushion.

'Stop it!'

'I'll take that.' Suddenly the TV remote was neatly whisked out of Vikram's hand. The twins' mum frowned at them. 'Neither of you should be watching anything at all. It's nearly time to leave for school.'

'Oh, Mum!' Vikram groaned. 'I went to school yesterday! I don't have to go again today, do I?'

Mum tried not to smile as she shook a warning finger at both of them. 'Go and get your school bags right away.'

'Mine's already by the front door,' Anita said smugly. Vikram stuck his tongue out at her and Anita giggled.

'Your lunch boxes are in the kitchen,' Mum went on. 'We're leaving in ten minutes and if you're not ready, there'll be trouble. I mean it.'

Vikram ran off to his bedroom to fetch his bag. Despite his complaints, he didn't really mind going to school. The sun was shining, a golden ball of fire in a blue, blue sky, but the morning air was still cool and fresh. It was nearly always hot and sunny in Goa, except for monsoon season when the rains were heavy enough to cause a deluge. And best of all, it was Friday. On Fridays the twins' teacher, Miss Pinto, took her class down to the beach to eat their lunch and play cricket.

Vikram and Anita always made sure they were on the same side for games. His twin sister could be a pain a lot of the time, but Vikram had to admit she was a great bowler. And he was a good batsman. Even though he and Anita fought like cat and dog sometimes, they made a brilliant team. Not just at cricket, but at everything. Unbeatable!

Vikram flipped his bag open quickly to check he hadn't forgotten anything. But inside there was no homework, no cricket ball, no pens or pencils and no mobile phone. Bewildered, he stared down at a wooden spoon, three onions and a plastic bag with a samosa inside it.

'Oh no!' Vikram groaned. 'MUM!' Clutching his school bag, he shot out of his bedroom.

* * *

When Anita hurried to the kitchen to retrieve her lunch box, she found Gran there, sitting at the table with a cup of tea in front of her and looking out of the window at the busy street five floors below their apartment. She was a tiny, grey-haired woman who was wrapped up warmly in a thick wool shawl, even though the sun was streaming through the glass.

'Hello, dear,' said Gran absently. She had a faraway expression on her face.

Anita greeted her in return and started looking around for the lunch boxes. She was keen to get to school today because they had a special Maths test, and Anita loved Maths. Vikram didn't, so Anita always helped him with his homework, and then Vikram helped her whenever they had spellings to learn. Anita was hopeless at spelling, but Vikram was always thinking up clever little ways to help her remember word patterns.

And it's Friday, Anita thought happily. *Lunch on the beach and a game of cricket. Yay!* She always enjoyed playing cricket on the same team as Vikram. It wasn't so bad being a twin, really, even though Vikram liked truly terrible TV programmes.

Anita finally spotted their lunch boxes stacked on top of each other in the corner of the kitchen counter. Mum had made coconut rice, fish curry and samosas yesterday evening, so they had particularly delicious leftovers for lunch today. Anita's mouth watered. Maybe she'd just nibble one corner of the crispy, spicy samosa right now, she decided.

Anita popped open the lid of her lunch box. Her eyes widened and her jaw dropped. There was no sign of curry, rice or samosa – just a cricket ball, a bunch of pens and pencils, and a notebook. The notebook was too big for the lunch box, and someone had bent it out of shape to cram it inside.

'Mum!' Anita wailed.

The twins' mum came rushing into the kitchen, trying to clip her earrings in at the same time. Vikram was close behind her, holding his school bag.

'My lunch has gone!' Anita said.

'So has the stuff from my school bag,' Vikram began. Then he caught sight of the cricket ball and pens inside his sister's lunch box, and the notebook squashed in beneath them, and groaned loudly in dismay.

'That's my homework!' Quickly Vikram grabbed the notebook and tried unsuccessfully to smooth out the pages. 'Miss Pinto's going to be so cross!'

The twins' gran got up from the table, looking worried.

'Did I do something wrong?' she asked in a trembling voice, grasping the edge of the table for support. 'I was just trying to help you both get ready for school.'

'No, Gran,' Anita said quickly. She hurried over to the table and helped her gran to sit down again. 'It's fine. Drink your tea. Nothing's wrong.'

The frown on Gran's face disappeared at once. She took a sip of tea and then smiled up at Anita. 'Thank you, Rajni.'

Anita smiled back, but didn't say anything about her gran calling her the wrong name. Rajni was Mum's name, but now that Gran was ill, she quite often muddled their names up.

'I'll ring Miss Pinto and explain,' Mum whispered to Vikram. 'Don't worry.'

Biting his lip, Vikram nodded. Although Gran had been ill for quite a while, he still hadn't got used to it. He hated seeing her like this. Mum and Dad had explained that, although Gran looked quite well, the illness had affected her mind, and especially her memory, over the last year or so. That was why sometimes Gran would forget things, or do something quite strange. Like putting Vikram's homework in Anita's lunch box.

'The thing is, Gran isn't going to get any better,' Dad had told them quietly. 'And she might even get worse. Later on, she may even completely forget who we are.'

'Can't the doctors make her better?' Anita had asked hopefully.

'No, they can't,' Mum had sighed, shaking her head. 'All we can do now is look after Gran and make her life as happy as possible.'

'But Gran doesn't act strange all the time,' Vikram had argued stubbornly. 'Sometimes she's exactly the same way she always was. So maybe she'll just get better all on her own?'

'She won't, son,' Dad had replied. 'We just have to accept it.'

Vikram couldn't bear to think that one day Gran might not remember who they were. Gran and Grandad had retired from work and moved in with Mum and Dad just before the twins were born. Grandad had died seven years ago, but throughout Vikram's life Gran had always been there, cooking delicious meals, reading them bedtime stories and teaching them how to play cricket. When Gran was a young girl, she'd played a lot of cricket with her older brothers, and it was from her Vikram had learned how to bat, and Anita had learned how to bowl really fast. But now when Vikram tried to talk to Gran about cricket, she struggled even to recall the rules of the game.

How could you just forget all those things? Vikram wondered as he stuffed the crumpled notebook into his school bag. *It wasn't fair. Why did this have to happen to our gran?*

Mum found the rest of Anita's lunch stowed away neatly in the fridge and a quick search revealed

Vikram's phone inside the washing machine which, fortunately, had not been switched on.

'That'll be Shanti,' Mum said as the doorbell rang. Shanti, their neighbour, arrived every morning to sit with Gran until Mum got back from work at lunchtime. She'd been coming for six months, ever since Gran had been left on her own and had taken the opportunity to have a bath. She'd left the cold tap running and almost flooded the apartment.

Gran looked confused. 'Who's Shanti?' she asked.

'Our neighbour,' Anita replied. 'She comes every morning, remember? She was here yesterday.' But Anita could see that at this moment Gran didn't remember, so she just patted her shoulder and ran to open the door. Anita recognized the expression on Vikram's face and knew exactly what her twin was thinking. No, it wasn't fair. Just like Vikram, Anita longed for Gran to be well again. But she was reconciled to the fact that it wasn't going to happen.

'Good morning, Anita.' Shanti, a big, jovial woman in a bright orange sari, breezed into the apartment. 'How's your gran?'

'She's fine, Auntie,' Anita replied, leading the way
to the kitchen. 'But I'm not sure she'll remember
who you are today.'

'Oh, hello Shanti,' Gran said with a smile, getting
up from the table. 'How nice of you to come and
visit me this morning. I haven't seen you for weeks.
How's your son Dilip getting on with his new job?'

Anita glanced at Vikram as Gran chatted with
Shanti. Although Gran had forgotten who Shanti
was a few moments ago, now she'd remembered
everything about their neighbour's family. It was

so strange how Gran's memory came and went. Strange, and rather scary.

'Would you like some tea?' Gran asked Shanti.

'Love some, but I'll make it,' Shanti said cheerfully. 'You sit down.'

'Goodbye, Gran.' Anita kissed her on the cheek. 'See you tonight.'

By now Vikram had finished packing his stuff back into his school bag. He crammed his lunch box in on top, first checking carefully that his lunch was inside.

'See you later, Gran.' Vikram leaned in to give her a hug, but to his surprise Gran gripped his arm tightly, pulled him towards her and whispered something in his ear.

'What did you say, Gran?' Vikram asked. Shanti was clattering about with the tea things and he hadn't heard a word.

'Don't forget about the treasure,' Gran replied urgently. 'Do you hear me, Vikram? You and Anita must find the family treasure and bring it back home.'

Chapter 2
A Key to the Mystery

'You must have got it all wrong, Vikram,' Anita scoffed, poking her brother in the ribs. 'There can't really be any treasure.'

It was lunchtime, and the twins were at the beach with the rest of their class. The midday sun was almost uncomfortably warm, but Miss Pinto and her students had found a shady spot near a cluster of palm trees to set up their cricket game. The beach was thronging with tourists from all over the world. They were luxuriating in the intense heat or paddling in the waves that broke in foamy ripples over the white sand. Further out, there were people swimming, snorkelling and surfing.

'I didn't get it wrong, Anita,' Vikram replied, annoyed. 'That was exactly what Gran said. Find the family treasure and bring it home.'

Anita rolled her eyes, but before she could say anything, it was time for Vikram to open the batting. As the team's best batsman, he always batted first.

As Vikram walked over to take his place in front of the cricket stumps, Anita frowned. Even if her brother hadn't made a mistake, it was still very unlikely that there was any treasure. Their gran had probably just mixed things up and got them all wrong, as she often did these days.

Vikram was thinking the same as he stood waiting for Rajesh to bowl the ball to him. *Maybe Gran had got confused again,* he thought. *But she'd sounded so certain, so sure …*

Vikram was so deep in thought, he didn't notice the ball come flying towards him. When he finally saw it, he lashed out wildly with the bat and sent the ball rocketing straight up into the air. Rajesh ran forward and caught it cleanly before it hit the sand.

'OUT!' called Miss Pinto, who was umpiring.

Everyone, including Anita, gasped with shock. Vikram was never out first ball. Sometimes he made it right to the end of the game without being out at all, and he always scored loads of runs. Not today, though.

Pink with embarrassment, Vikram hurried back and surrendered the bat to his teammate Sunita who was next in line. 'Sorry, everyone,' he mumbled.

'I suppose you got distracted because you're still thinking about the treasure?' Anita said with a sigh as the game resumed.

Vikram nodded. 'I know Gran gets things mixed up sometimes,' he replied slowly. 'But this time I think she meant what she said. It would be totally brilliant if there really was some hidden treasure somewhere, Anita!'

'Just because you want something to be true, doesn't mean it is true.'

Vikram grimaced. 'You sound really grown-up and boring!' he teased. 'We've got to check it out, Anita. Think about it – a chest full of gold and jewels and diamonds and stuff, just waiting for us to find it!'

'Did Gran say anything about gold, diamonds and jewels?' Anita raised her eyebrows incredulously.

'No, but that's what treasure is in stories, isn't it? It belonged to Gran and Grandad, and now Gran wants us to find it for her.'

Anita didn't look very convinced. 'But where would Gran and Grandad have got the treasure from?' she asked. 'They never had much money. Mum said Grandad was a driver before he retired, and Gran used to be a nanny and look after little children. How could they have loads of treasure? And even if they did, then why is it lost?'

'How should I know?' Vikram said impatiently. 'Oh, I can't wait to get home tonight and ask Gran some more questions!'

The twins watched as Sunita was bowled out, having scored only eight runs.

'I think we're going to lose today,' Anita predicted.

'Who cares?' Vikram laughed. 'We've got more important things to think about!'

* * *

'I can't believe we managed to win that game after all,' Vikram said as he rang the doorbell of the family apartment later that afternoon. 'You bowled out six of the other team before they even scored a single run. You were ace, Anita!'

'I know,' Anita giggled. 'Gran taught me how to put loads of spin on the ball.'

'Before she got ill, you mean.' Vikram sighed. 'Shall we ask her about the treasure tonight?'

Anita hesitated. 'Let's wait and see how she is first. We don't want her to get all worried and confused.'

The front door opened and Gran peered out. For a moment she looked a little perplexed, then her face cleared and she smiled. 'Here you are. Come in –

your mum's just making a phone call. And I've been making coconut pancakes for you.'

'Oh, yum!' Vikram said, licking his lips. They dumped their bags in the hall and raced to the kitchen. Vikram won, and his prize was to swipe the first pancake from the tottering pile on the plate. Anita was close behind and as they both munched their pancakes, Vikram glanced at his twin. Gran seemed OK. She was taking mugs out of the cupboard to make tea. Maybe now was a good time to ask her about the treasure.

'Gran, do you remember what you said to me this morning?' he asked. 'Before I went to school?' Anita shook her head at him, but Vikram pressed on.

'You said we had to find the family treasure,' he prompted.

'What treasure?' Gran asked. She wasn't looking at Vikram. Instead she was staring intently at the kettle.

'I don't know, Gran. We were hoping you could tell us.'

Suddenly an expression of distress swept over Gran's face like a wave. 'I can't remember how to switch the kettle on!' she gasped, and tears began to roll down her cheeks.

'Don't worry, Gran.' Anita sprang forward, throwing Vikram a warning look. 'This is how you do it. See?'

'Is everything all right?' Mum came out of the living room clutching her phone.

'Yes, me and Gran are just making tea,' Anita said quickly.

When Mum and Gran had gone into the living room with their tea, Vikram and Anita sat down at the kitchen table to start their homework.

'I feel really bad now,' Vikram said, biting his lip. 'I didn't mean to upset Gran.'

'It wasn't you, Vik,' Anita replied gently. 'It was because she'd forgotten how to switch the kettle on.'

'She didn't remember telling me about the treasure either,' Vikram sighed.

'I've been wondering,' Anita said thoughtfully. 'Maybe Gran's thinking about her gold wedding jewellery. That could be what she means by treasure. Maybe she's forgotten she keeps it in the safe in Dad's study.'

But Vikram was shaking his head. 'No, she told me to find the family treasure and bring it home. That means it's somewhere else, not here.'

'But Gran does get mixed up,' Anita reminded him quietly. 'It's no good, Vikram. I think we should forget all about the treasure. Come on. Let's get our homework done and then we'll have the whole weekend free.'

Vikram looked disappointed, but he grudgingly did as Anita suggested and started his homework. He was testing Anita on the spellings for Monday's test when Gran wandered into the kitchen.

'The man who makes elephants,' Gran murmured to herself.

Vikram and Anita stared at each other, puzzled.

'The man who makes elephants,' Gran repeated quietly. 'At the beach market. That's where the family treasure is. He's keeping it safe for me.'

'The man who makes elephants is looking after the treasure for you, Gran?' Vikram asked, jumping to his feet in excitement.

'What's his name?' Anita wanted to know. 'Does he have a stall at the beach market?'

Gran didn't reply. She put her hand into the pocket of her cardigan and took out an old metal key. 'What's this?' she asked, looking confused.

'Is it for Anita and me, Gran?' Vikram could hardly get the words out, he was so thrilled. 'Is it the key to the treasure chest?'

Gran handed the key to Vikram and wandered out of the kitchen again.

'I knew it!' Triumphantly, Vikram waved the key in front of Anita's nose. 'I knew there really was some family treasure somewhere – and we're the ones who are going to find it!'

Chapter 3
Market Day

'Now you know how busy the beach market gets with all those tourists,' Mum called as Anita and Vikram hurried out of the apartment early the following morning. 'Make sure you stick by Shanti's side and don't go wandering off and getting lost.'

'We won't, Mum.' Anita closed the door behind them with a click.

'It's lucky Shanti runs a food stall at the beach market,' Vikram said as they headed to Shanti's apartment. 'Mum would never have let us go there on our own.'

The beach market wasn't often visited by Vikram and Anita's family or the other locals because it was actually a tourist market that sold all kinds of souvenirs. The last time the twins had been there was three years ago when their cousins had visited from Delhi.

'I wonder how difficult it will be to find the man who makes elephants,' Anita frowned, ringing Shanti's doorbell.

'Not difficult at all,' Vikram replied cheerfully. 'We're going to find the treasure today. I just know it!'

The door opened.

'Ah, here are my two assistants.' Shanti beamed at them. 'I'm almost ready. I just need a little help carrying these baskets down to my car.'

She loaded a couple of baskets on to Anita's shoulders and two more on to Vikram's. They staggered a little under the weight.

'What's inside, Auntie?' Vikram asked. 'They're really heavy!'

'All the ingredients I need to make my snacks,' Shanti replied briskly. 'Onions, potatoes, spices, lentils, oil, flour, chutney and lots more.' She picked up the remaining three big baskets herself and shoved a huge bunch of coriander on top of one of them.

'Right, let's go. All the cooking equipment is already packed into my car.'

'So,' Shanti went on as they trudged to the lift, 'your mum says you're doing a project about the tourist market at school?'

'Er – yes,' Anita replied. It had been Vikram's idea to tell their mum that. Vikram had persuaded Anita that they would tell their parents once they had found the treasure. It would be an amazing surprise!

The twins squeezed into the back of Shanti's car, contorting themselves around all the baskets and the cooking equipment, and off they went. The beach market was about half an hour's drive from their apartment block. Although it was still quite early, a steady stream of traders and shoppers was already building up.

'Here we are.' Shanti manoeuvred the car carefully past a big white house that stood right next to the market entrance. 'We need to hurry. There are crowds of tourists arriving already.'

Anita and Vikram helped Shanti to unload the car, struggling under the weight of the baskets and cooking equipment. It seemed like a long trek to her stall on the beach. This beach stretched for miles, its pale golden sand glowing in the bright sunshine, but the twins thought the small beach not far from their apartment block was much nicer and quieter.

It was fun to see the market coming to life though. The whole area was already full of bustling energy as the sellers ran around setting out their wares. Some were laying out silver jewellery on blue velvet cloths, while others were draping bedspreads embroidered with tiny mirrors over the tops of their stalls so that they fluttered in the sea breeze. Others were setting up tables piled with carved wooden flutes, tabla drums, string puppets with painted faces, saris, T-shirts, beachwear, flip-flops and leather sandals. Dotted throughout the market were lots of stalls selling a mouth-watering variety of food, and hot and cold drinks.

Both Vikram and Anita were fascinated to watch all this unfolding before their very eyes, but for the first hour or two Shanti kept them too busy to concentrate on enjoying the scene. They helped her to lay out all the food she'd made at home so that it looked enticing for the customers. Shanti's daughter, Kareena, was there with her little boy, Ricky, so the twins played with him while Shanti and Kareena set up the cooking equipment. Soon the delicious aroma of samosas frying attracted more and more customers to the stall, and the twins helped to wrap food for the customers and take the money.

'There are loads of different people here,' Anita

whispered to Vikram as a mother and father with three children stopped to buy some snacks. They were speaking a language neither of the twins recognized.

'They're Russian,' Shanti explained when the family had paid and moved on. 'There are lots of English, German and American tourists here too.'

'Shanti, can Anita and I go and have a look around the market now?' Vikram asked eagerly. He was bursting to get out from behind the stall and search for the man Gran had told them about.

But to Vikram's dismay, Shanti shook her head. 'Your mum said you weren't allowed to go off on your own. But when we've cooked some fresh food, I'm going to walk around the market and look for customers, so you can come with me.'

'Brilliant!' Vikram was all smiles again.

The twins waited impatiently as Shanti and Kareena began cooking again. They helped Shanti load a tray with all the goodies and then, at last, they were ready.

'Now, make sure you stay right next to me,' Shanti ordered, picking up the tray. 'I don't want to go home and tell your mum that I've lost you!'

'We will, won't we, Vikram?'

'Course we will,' Vikram agreed at once.
He just wanted to get on with the treasure hunt!

The three of them set off, leaving Kareena in
charge of the stall. But their progress was very slow
because Shanti kept stopping to sell her food to the
other stallholders, as well as to the shoppers. It took
them a very long time just to get to the end of the
row where Shanti's stall was situated.

'And look, there are about twenty more rows of
stalls!' Vikram wailed, dancing around impatiently

as Shanti handed over some bhajis and prawn rissoles to a man selling T-shirts. There was no way of stopping Shanti from chattering away to her customers, which made Vikram even more anxious. He knew Shanti loved to talk, and he also knew that the market began to close down around midday. 'We're never going to have time to look around all the stalls properly.'

'We can always come back with Shanti next Saturday,' said Anita. 'If we think it's worth it.'

'Next Saturday?' Vikram looked horrified.

'No way! I want to find the treasure today. And what do you mean, if it's worth it?' he added, rolling his eyes at Anita. 'This is treasure we're talking about!'

Finally Shanti finished her conversation and the twins followed her into the next row of stalls.

'Shanti!' called one of the stallholders, a woman selling glass bangles in a dazzling array of juicy fruit colours. 'How are you? And how's your grandson?'

'Ricky's with Kareena on my stall,' Shanti replied with a smile. 'He's doing fine – happy and healthy! And how are your children, Dipti?'

'Oh no, Shanti could be talking for hours again!' Vikram whispered to Anita. 'You know what she's like. She never stops!'

It was then that Anita noticed something very intriguing. 'Why don't you stop talking and look over there?' she said, gesturing to the stall opposite.

Vikram looked and his heart began to pound so hard that he felt dizzy. The man sitting behind the stall was selling carved wooden animals.

And right at the front was a long procession of elephants.

Chapter 4
A Procession of Elephants

'It's – it's him!' Vikram gasped. 'That's the man who makes elephants. We've found him!'

He was about to race over to the stall when Anita caught his arm. 'Hold on,' she said. 'We can't just go rushing off. Remember what Mum and Shanti said.'

'But it's right there!' Vikram begged. 'We'll only be two metres away!'

Anita shook her head warningly. Still hanging on to him to stop him from running off, she tapped Shanti on the shoulder. 'Auntie, is it OK if we go and look at the carved animals?' she asked.

'Of course,' Shanti agreed, 'But you mustn't go any further into the market on your own. Is that clear? I'll be keeping my eye on you!'

'Thanks, Auntie.' Anita released Vikram's arm and he cannoned off towards the elephant stall, dodging around the shoppers as he went.

'Ah, good morning,' the man behind the stall said cheerfully. 'I can see you love my elephants. You have great taste, my boy! Which one would you like?'

'Sorry, I don't want to buy an elephant,' Vikram
explained quickly. 'I just wanted to ask if you knew
our gran.'

'Of course I do,' the man replied. 'Now, which
of my beautiful elephants would you like to buy?'

'I never said Gran's name – I don't think he
knows her at all,' Vikram whispered to Anita.

'No, he doesn't,' Anita agreed. 'He just wants
us to buy something.'

'Look, this is my most beautiful, most expensive
elephant,' the stallholder was saying. He showed
the twins a big elephant painted with swirling red
and gold patterns. 'They are all handmade and
hand-painted. I'll give you a very good price!'

'Sorry, but we don't want to buy an elephant,'
Anita said politely. 'We just wanted to ask you if
you knew our gran, that's all.'

The twins edged away from the stall, back to Shanti, who had been keeping a close eye on what was happening.

'So what are you two up to?' she demanded.

'Oh, nothing, Auntie,' Anita muttered.

'Really?' Shanti raised her eyebrows. 'Well, I think there's something going on and you'd better tell me what the secret is. Otherwise I shall take you both home this minute!'

'No, don't do that!' Vikram said quickly. So he and Anita told Shanti the whole story, about how Gran had told them to find the family treasure. They explained how Gran had told them about the man who made elephants at the beach market and they showed her the old metal key.

'So you really think there might be some treasure?' Shanti asked dubiously.

Anita simply shrugged, not even sure she believed it herself, but Vikram nodded. 'Yes,' he said eagerly, 'and all we have to do is find it!'

'And what do you think this treasure might be?'

'Well, gold and jewels and stuff,' Vikram replied. Shanti looked even more doubtful.

'Auntie, are there any other stalls in the market that sell elephants?' asked Vikram.

Shanti nodded.

'Yes!' Vikram high-fived Anita triumphantly. 'See? I told you we'd find the treasure today! We just got the wrong man, that's all.'

'Can you take us to the other stall, Auntie?' Anita asked. Vikram was hopping around on the spot, desperate to start their search again.

Shanti shook her head. 'Calm down for just one moment!' she said. 'There are at least eight other stalls that sell elephants at this market.'

'EIGHT!' Anita repeated, wide-eyed.

'No way!' Vikram gasped.

Shanti nodded. 'And there might be a few more I don't know about,' she added. 'The stalls change every couple of weeks.'

Vikram glanced at Anita in despair, and Anita felt a pang of sympathy for her twin. He was so determined to find the treasure, but Anita was beginning to think it was just a wild goose chase. They couldn't really trust anything Gran said when she was so confused and muddled half the time.

'Listen, I'll tell you exactly what we're going to do,' Shanti said with a smile. 'We'll carry on walking up and down all these rows of stalls, and I'll sell my snacks, and you can talk to the stallholders. If the man who knows your gran is here, we'll find him if it's the last thing we do!'

Vikram cheered so loudly that people turned to look at them and smiled.

'Let's go, Auntie!' he said.

So they set off again, the twins scouring the area for the next stall that sold carved elephants. One by one they found the stalls, and each time Anita and Vikram asked the same question: 'Do you know our gran, Mrs Meera Sharma?'

But every time the stallholder would say, 'No!'

'Never mind,' Shanti said gently as they wound their way back to her stall. 'Maybe your gran just got confused. It's a lovely idea to think there might be some secret treasure somewhere out there, just waiting to be found. But really, if you think about it, it doesn't seem very likely, does it?'

'No, Auntie,' Vikram sighed.

Anita felt sorry for Vikram, but there was

nothing more they could do. And he hadn't *really* thought they'd find it, had he?

They arrived back at the food stall, and Shanti went to talk to her daughter and give her grandson a cuddle.

'You know what?' Vikram whispered in Anita's ear. 'I'm not giving up just yet!'

Anita glanced at her twin in surprise. She'd thought that would be the end of it but Vikram had a very obstinate look on his face, an expression that Anita recognized. Their gran used to say that Vikram was as stubborn as a donkey once he got an idea into his head.

Vikram held up the key that Gran had given him. 'This must be the key to Gran's treasure chest, or why else would she have given it to me? The treasure's out there somewhere, and somehow I'm going to find it. I don't know how – I just need a few more clues.'

'*We're* going to find it!' Anita declared, suddenly feeling fired up again by Vikram's enthusiasm. 'Maybe Gran will have some more information for us. We'll keep trying!'

Chapter 5
Animals in the Sand

Vikram and Anita's spirits rallied once they'd made the decision to continue their search for the treasure. They munched the onion bhajis that Kareena gave them and people-watched for a while. But before long, the crowds of shoppers began to dissipate, and some of the stallholders started packing away their goods.

'The market's coming to an end now,' Shanti said. 'Time to go home.'

Vikram and Anita were helping Shanti and Kareena to wrap up the remaining food when Shanti's phone buzzed.

'I've had a text from your mum,' Shanti told the twins. 'She and your dad and your gran are coming to collect you, and you're all going to have a picnic on the beach here.'

'Cool!' Vikram exclaimed.

'Will you stay as well?' Anita asked.

Shanti shook her head. 'No, thank you, Anita. We need to get this little one home now for his afternoon nap.' She tickled Ricky under his little chin. 'But I'm sure you'll have a lovely afternoon on the beach.'

They'd almost finished packing away Shanti's stall when Anita spotted Dad, Mum and Gran weaving their way towards them through the last straggling shoppers. Mum was arm in arm with Gran so that she didn't wander off and get lost, while Dad was carrying a cool box, a parasol and some baskets of food.

'Thanks for letting us come with you today, Shanti,' Anita said. 'The market is so exciting.'

'We had a great time!' Vikram added.

'Even though you didn't find any treasure?' Shanti said, eyes twinkling.

'Don't say anything to our mum and dad about that, will you, Auntie?' Anita asked a little anxiously.

Shanti put a finger to her lips. 'Don't worry,' she murmured. 'I won't say a single word. And don't forget, you two, treasure isn't just gold and jewels, you know.'

What does she mean by that? Vikram wondered.

'Hello, it's the twin terrors!' Dad joked as he, Mum and Gran arrived at Shanti's stall. 'All ready for a picnic on the beach?'

'Yum! Of course we are!'

'You're always ready for food, Vik!' Anita teased.

'Well, I hope you didn't eat all of Shanti's profits,' Mum said with a smile. 'Have they behaved themselves, Shanti?'

'They've been as good as gold,' Shanti replied. She grinned at Vikram and Anita. 'Little treasures, in fact!'

The twins exchanged glances and laughed, somewhat to their parents' bemusement.

'Well, we must go home and put Ricky down for his nap,' Shanti said. Kareena had picked Ricky up and he was already looking sleepy. 'Have a lovely picnic.'

Gran was staring at the baby. 'Shanti, is that your son, Dilip?' she asked, frowning.

'No, Dilip's all grown up now,' Shanti explained gently. 'This is my grandson, Ricky.'

'Ricky,' Gran repeated, as if she was trying to fix the name in her mind. Anita went over and took Gran's other arm and they all waved to Shanti, Kareena and the baby as they headed off through the crowds towards the beach.

Many of the tourists who'd come to visit the market had stayed to sunbathe, swim and surf, so there was hardly a free centimetre of sand on which to spread their picnic.

'It's too hot for Gran to sit in the sun,' Mum said. 'We must find somewhere to put up our parasol.'

They pressed on a little further and soon came to a less crowded spot. Dad busied himself with the parasol and Mum laid out a blanket for everyone to sit on. Meanwhile, Vikram peered impatiently into one of the baskets of food.

'I'm starving. What's for lunch?'

Mum and Dad had packed some of their favourite things: chicken and cheese wraps, juicy tomatoes, and cucumber and onion salad. There were pineapple and mango smoothies to drink, and syrupy sponge cakes for pudding. *It's lovely to sit outside to eat lunch: much better than being indoors,* Anita thought. Although the delicious shade was lapping coolly over them, they could still feel the warmth of the sun and watch the waves rolling up on to the beach. Gran was enjoying it too, Anita could see. She'd eaten much more than she usually did at home, and now she was dozing a little.

'Are there any wraps left?' Vikram asked, searching the baskets one by one with an air of disappointment.

'No,' Mum replied. 'You've eaten them all.'

'You can't still be hungry, Vikram,' Anita said with a grin.

'Tell you what,' Dad offered. 'Give me twenty minutes to read my newspaper, and then we'll go and get some ice cream. How's that?'

'Thanks, Dad,' Vikram beamed.

As good as his word, a while later Dad folded up his newspaper and he, Vikram and Anita set off along the beach to the nearest ice cream shop about five minutes' walk away. Gran had fallen asleep under the parasol so Mum said she'd stay behind and pack up the picnic, then she and Gran would drive to the ice cream shop to meet them.

The twins paddled in the edge of the sea as they walked, relishing the sensation of the warm, frothy waves breaking over their toes.

'It's a shame we didn't find the treasure today,' Anita remarked. 'But maybe Gran might remember something else, and give us another clue.' She glanced cautiously over her shoulder at their dad who was just behind them, hoping he wasn't listening to their conversation. But a few moments ago Dad had met a friend who worked in the same office and they were chatting as they walked along, so the twins could talk without being overheard.

'Today isn't over yet,' Vikram pointed out. 'There's still time!'

They'd reached the ice cream shop by now, but Dad and his friend were still chatting and the twins were reluctant to interrupt. So they hung around, waiting politely for a pause in the conversation. Then suddenly Anita noticed a commotion of some sort further along the beach. She could see that, for some reason, a crowd had gathered.

Anita nudged Vikram. 'I wonder what all those people are looking at?'

Dad's friend, Manjit, overheard her. 'Oh, that'll be the sand sculptor. He's here every weekend in the same spot. His sand sculptures are brilliant. He always draws a crowd.'

'Dad, can we go and check it out?' Vikram asked eagerly. A sand sculptor sounded amazing – even better than ice cream!

'OK,' Dad agreed. 'We can buy our ice creams on the way back.'

So they continued along the beach past the ice cream shop and towards the crowd of people. Vikram and Anita were so keen to see the sand sculptures, they kept getting ahead of Dad and Manjit and had to stop and wait impatiently for them to catch up. But at last they came close enough to get a glimpse of what all the other people were looking at – although there was such a crowd that the twins both had to stand on tiptoe in order to see over people's shoulders.

'Wow!' Vikram gasped. 'They *are* amazing!'

The sand had been sculpted into beautiful and detailed figures of animals. Some of the figures were life-size – a dolphin, a dog, a monkey and a group of cats and kittens. Others had been made bigger than life-size – there was a gargantuan frog, a sinister-looking giant crab, a mammoth snail with a curved shell, and a shoal of huge fish swimming through the sand. There were also models of much bigger animals, and Vikram identified a lion, a tiger and a hippo.

'Look – that's really clever,' Vikram said, pointing the hippo out to Anita. Only the top half of the hippo's body could be seen, just as if the bottom half of it was submerged in the water and it was swimming around. 'How does the sand stick together like that to make all these animal shapes?'

'Don't you remember how we made sandcastles when we were little?' Anita reminded him with a grin. 'We used to put sand in the bucket and pour the water on top, and that would make the sand stick together. Then, when we turned the bucket over, it would come out in one piece.'

'These sand animals are loads more difficult than just making a sandcastle!' Vikram pointed out. At that moment the crowd in front of them thinned out a little as a group of people turned to leave, and the twins found themselves right at the front with a much better view of the sand sculptures. Now, for the first time, they saw the young sculptor. He was sitting on the sand, surrounded by buckets of water and working with intense concentration on a figure of another animal.

'It's an elephant!' Vikram and Anita gasped at exactly the same moment.

The young man was putting the finishing touches to a life-size baby elephant, defining its ears and mouth with a stick. He had a plastic container in front of him and people were throwing in coins and notes as they walked past.

'Do you think this could be the man Gran was talking about?' Vikram whispered.

'He doesn't just make elephants though, does he?' Anita pointed out gently, so as not to dash Vikram's hopes. 'He makes all sorts of animals. And besides, he looks too young to know Gran.'

'It's worth a try though, isn't it?' Vikram said eagerly. He turned to their father who was standing behind them discussing the sand sculptures with Manjit. 'Dad, can we give the sculptor some money, please?'

Dad got out his wallet and gave Vikram some coins. Then the twins hurried across the sand towards the young man. He'd just finished the elephant and had stood up, brushing the sand from his clothes.

'The elephant looks great!' Vikram said, placing the money in the container.

'Thank you,' the young man said with a smile.

'What sand animal do you like making best?' Anita asked curiously.

'Oh, I love making elephants,' the young man replied, emptying the money from the container into his bag. 'I make different animals every week, but there's always an elephant in there somewhere.'

Vikram and Anita exchanged delighted glances. That was the right answer, as far as they were concerned!

'We think you might know our gran,' Vikram said. He could hardly blurt the words out, he was so tongue-tied with excitement. 'She's called Mrs Meera Sharma.'

The young man frowned thoughtfully. 'I think I know that name ... ' The twins glanced at each other hopefully. Then the young man's face lit up. 'Ah, yes! She's a friend of my mother's.'

Vikram and Anita were thrilled.

'Well, the thing is—' Vikram began, but just then Dad tapped him on the shoulder.

'We need to go and get those ice creams now, son,' Dad said. 'Your mum and gran have come to meet us.'

The twins looked over and saw their family car parked nearby on the beach road. Mum waved at them as she helped Gran out of the car.

'That's our gran over there,' Anita told the sculptor.

The young man shaded his eyes from the sun and stared at Gran. 'Sorry,' he said with a shrug. 'That's not my mum's friend.'

'Are you sure?' Vikram asked, despondency flooding through him once again.

The young man nodded. 'My mum's friend is quite a bit younger. They must just have the same name, that's all.'

Vikram felt so deflated, he couldn't speak. But Anita had had an idea.

'We're searching for a man who makes elephants,' she explained. 'Do you know anyone?'

The young man stared at her, nonplussed. He thought for a moment before a slow smile spread across his face.

'Actually, yes, I do. Can you see that big white house at the entrance to the tourist market?' He turned and pointed to the house in the distance. Vikram and Anita nodded. They remembered seeing the house when they'd arrived at the market with Shanti earlier that morning. 'Well, the man who owns that house is an artist,' the sand sculptor went on. 'He paints pictures of elephants and also sculpts them in marble. He mainly lives in America now, and he's become very rich and famous in the last few years. Maybe he could be the man you're looking for?'

'OK, thank you.' Anita and Vikram turned to leave, trooping after their dad across the beach.

'The owner of the big white house can't be the man we're looking for,' Vikram said gloomily. 'How would Gran know somebody so rich and famous?'

'It's another dead end,' Anita sighed. Her earlier enthusiasm had now faded somewhat, and once again she was beginning to think their treasure hunt was doomed to failure.

They all went to the shop to buy their ice creams, and the twins' disappointment lifted a little as they chose their favourite flavours: banana for Vikram and strawberry for Anita.

'Are we going home now, Mum?' Vikram asked, struggling to lick fast enough to stop the sticky ice cream dripping off the cone and running down his arm.

'Not straight away,' Mum replied. 'We're going to visit Rakesh and Esha. They haven't seen Gran for ages, and they've invited us to stop by for a cup of tea.'

Vikram and Anita were pleased. Rakesh and Esha owned a spice plantation which was an intriguing place to explore and every time they visited, there was something new and interesting to see. The couple were old friends of Gran's and always made a big fuss of them.

'I hope there's cake for tea,' Vikram said as they all climbed back into the car.

'If you eat any more, you'll burst!' Anita giggled, fastening her seat belt and then helping Gran to clip hers into place.

'Right, off we go to the spice plantation,' Dad said as he started the car.

'The treasure is there,' Gran said in a low voice. She was perched alertly on the back seat, staring out of the window at the beach. Anita, who was next to Gran, heard what she said and almost jumped out of her skin. Quickly she leaned in closer.

'What did you say about the spice plantation, Gran?' Anita whispered.

'The treasure is there,' Gran repeated softly, still staring out of the car window. 'The family treasure is there.'

Chapter 6
At the Spice Plantation

Anita was surprised and baffled by her gran's words. She didn't know what to think. First Gran had said the man who made elephants was keeping the treasure safe. Now Gran was saying that the treasure was at Rakesh and Esha's spice plantation!

Anita waited until they arrived before she told Vikram, just in case their parents overheard. As they climbed out of the car and Rakesh, Esha and their four dogs rushed out of the house to greet them, Anita whispered to Vikram exactly what Gran had said.

'It's here?' Vikram gasped in amazement.

'Yes, here you are!' Rakesh beamed at the twins, not quite hearing what Vikram had said. He was a short, cheerful man who was always cracking jokes. 'It's been too long since we saw you all.'

'Far too long,' his wife Esha agreed, drawing Vikram and Anita into a hug. 'Now, would you like to have tea first, or shall we show you around? We've expanded our business quite a lot since you were last here. We've started growing many different spices.'

'Please can we look around before tea?' Vikram burst out eagerly, patting the dogs as they crowded around him, wagging their tails exuberantly. Now he knew the treasure was definitely here, Vikram was eager to start scouring the place for it.

'No cake first?' Rakesh asked him teasingly.

'We've just had lunch and ice cream,' Mum explained, 'so I think we're ready for a walk now. We'd love to look around.'

'Well, as long as Meera is feeling well enough.' Esha tucked her arm into Gran's and gave her a squeeze. 'We'll only take a short walk.'

'I'll be fine,' Gran replied. 'It's good to see you again, Esha.'

Anita was glad to see that Gran had remembered that Rakesh and Esha were her friends. The grown-ups set off slowly, with Vikram and Anita scurrying impatiently along just in front of them. The dogs came too, bounding around everyone in their excitement at having visitors.

'What did Gran say exactly?' Vikram asked Anita. He kept his voice low so the others couldn't hear.

'Gran said, "The treasure is there," when Dad was talking about the spice plantation,' Anita told him.

Vikram looked very confused. 'But what about the man who makes elephants?' he asked. 'Rakesh doesn't make elephants – he grows spices!'

Anita shrugged. 'I don't know,' she replied. 'Maybe Gran is getting a bit muddled again.'

The grounds of the spice plantation were lush and green and alive with wonderful tropical, exotic scents. Parakeets and butterflies fluttered around the twins as they walked through the trees. There were tall cashew-nut trees and palm trees with monkeys chasing each other playfully from branch to branch and hanging upside down by their tails. Rakesh and Esha had recently started growing fruit as well as spices – pineapples, bananas, melons, grapes and figs. But there were more spice plants than anything else, including ginger, cinnamon, nutmeg, chillies, cloves, and vanilla – with its long green pods hanging from the vine.

'Did you know that vanilla is the second most expensive spice in the whole world?' Rakesh asked, opening up one of the pods and showing the twins the tiny black seeds inside.

'What's the most expensive?' Vikram asked.

'Saffron,' Esha replied. 'We've started growing that too. It comes from a crocus flower. We'll show you our crocus farm next.'

After the crocus farm, Rakesh and Esha took them into one of the big warehouses where the workers were sorting and drying the spices.

Although Vikram and Anita were enjoying their tour of the spice plantation, they didn't forget to keep their eyes open for possible hiding places where Gran's treasure might be concealed. Anita didn't think it was very likely that they would find it hidden in the spice plantation among the trees and plants, though. Nor in the warehouses where one of the workers might stumble across it. Maybe their gran had got it wrong again ...

Vikram was thinking the same thing. He was a lot less excited than he'd been earlier when Anita first told him what Gran had said. Was the treasure really here? Vikram was beginning to feel very sure that it wasn't.

'Maybe Rakesh and Esha are keeping the treasure safe for Gran somewhere,' Anita suggested hopefully, as they made their way back to the big wooden house for afternoon tea.

'But they've never said anything about it, and we've been here lots of times before,' Vikram pointed out. 'So why haven't Rakesh and Esha told Mum and Dad about the treasure if it is here?'

'Maybe Gran left it here in their house ages ago and they've just forgotten about it,' Anita suggested.

'The key Gran gave me is really big,' Vikram said, feeling the shape of the key in his pocket. 'So the treasure chest must be big too. If it's inside their house, they can't just have forgotten about it!'

'We could ask them,' Anita said.

Vikram grimaced. 'I suppose we could,' he muttered unenthusiastically. 'But it'd be much more exciting to find the treasure ourselves.'

The table had been laid for tea on the verandah of the house, and everyone, including Vikram and Anita, sat down. The housekeeper brought the tea tray, some orange juice for the twins and three different kinds of cake – vanilla sponge, cinnamon cake and a ginger loaf.

'All made with our own spices,' Rakesh explained proudly.

'Can I try a bit of each?' Vikram asked eagerly, and everyone laughed.

After some thought, Anita chose the vanilla sponge and savoured the sweet flavour of the spice. While she was eating it, she kept glancing around, alert for places where a treasure chest might be hidden. It was then that she noticed a cluster of rickety old wooden buildings close by the house, half-concealed by a clump of palm trees.

'Uncle, what are those buildings over there?' she asked. She'd seen them before, she remembered, but had never been bothered to ask any questions about them.

'Oh, those are our old warehouses,' Rakesh replied as he sipped his tea. 'We built new ones about five years ago – the new warehouses are those you visited today. They're much bigger because we needed a lot more space to sort the spices.'

'I'm afraid those old warehouses have become rather a dumping-ground for all our junk,' Esha laughed. 'I can't remember half of what's in there! We use them to store stuff there isn't room for in the house, like old furniture. Chairs, tables, dressers, chests—'

'Chests?' Vikram blurted out, all ears. But he'd just bitten into a piece of ginger loaf and a crumb of it went down the wrong way. He started to cough and choke and had to take a quick glug of orange juice.

'Are you all right, Vik?' Anita asked, patting her brother on the back. She knew exactly why he was suddenly showing such an interest in the contents of the old warehouses.

'I'm fine,' Vikram managed, taking another swig of orange juice. 'Um – Auntie – is it OK if Anita and I go for a little walk?'

'Of course,' Esha agreed kindly. 'Just stay close and make sure you can always see the house. It's very safe here, but it's easy to get lost in the plantation.'

'Make sure you do what Esha says,' Mum added.

Anita and Vikram climbed down from the verandah and strolled towards the old warehouses, trying not to betray their eagerness by rushing.

'These old buildings sound like the perfect place to find a treasure chest!' Vikram's irrepressible excitement was mounting once more.

'Yes, and maybe that's why Rakesh and Esha have forgotten that Gran left her treasure here,' Anita remarked, waving at the gardener who was watering the plants nearby. The twins had met him several times before, and he waved back at them. 'It might have got mixed up with all the junk.'

However, the first warehouse was a big disappointment. The door was hanging half off its hinges, so the twins could easily peep inside. The warehouse smelt of musty old spices and it was full of empty sacks and broken tools.

'Let's try the next one,' Anita said.

The door to the next warehouse was closed. Vikram went to open it, but Anita stopped him.

'We shouldn't go inside without asking Rakesh and Esha,' she said.

'I bet it isn't locked,' Vikram said longingly. Then he noticed a hole in the wood about halfway up the door. Vikram glanced at the gardener who was watering plants not far off, just to make sure that he wasn't watching them. Then quickly he stood on tiptoe and peered through the hole.

This warehouse was full of old furniture, just as Esha had said. And right away Vikram spotted a big, battered wooden chest sitting on the floor.

'Anita, I think I've found it!' Vikram gasped, unable to believe his eyes. 'I've found the chest with the family treasure!'

'Let me see.' Anita pushed Vikram aside and took a look through the hole for herself.

Vikram's right, she thought excitedly. The chest looked old and mysterious. It had brass hinges and a large brass keyhole that seemed like it might be of the right dimensions to fit the key Gran had given Vikram.

'We need to get inside!' Vikram exclaimed, jumping up and down with glee. The gardener had stopped watering the plants and was watching them curiously but Vikram was far too thrilled to care. 'Let me try the door, Anita. I bet Rakesh and Esha wouldn't mind if we went in.'

Before Anita could reply, they heard footsteps. The housekeeper appeared through the palm trees. She smiled as she walked past them to the warehouse door, opened it and went in, leaving the door wide open.

'See, I told you it wasn't locked!' Vikram nudged Anita. 'Ask her if we can have a look inside.'

'No, you ask her!' Anita whispered back.

The housekeeper went straight up to the treasure chest, and the twins watched in amazement as she lifted the lid.

'The chest wasn't locked either,' Vikram murmured to Anita. He wondered if the housekeeper was planning to steal Gran's treasure. But surely she wouldn't try to take it right in front of them?

The lid of the treasure chest fell open. Vikram and Anita's mouths fell open too. The chest was packed to the top with what looked like ragged old towels and dishcloths. The housekeeper took out a couple of cloths and then closed the lid again. She looked surprised to see the twins watching her as she retreated towards the door.

'We were wondering what was inside that chest,' Anita explained quickly. 'It looks really old.'

'Yes, I think your Auntie Esha brought it with her from her family home when she moved here, after she got married,' the housekeeper explained. 'We keep all our old towels and cleaning cloths in there now.'

Vikram and Anita glanced at each other, embarrassment washing over them.

'I think your parents will be ready to leave soon,' the housekeeper told the twins as she headed back towards the house. 'I'll pack up some cake for you to take home.'

'Thank you very much,' Vikram mumbled. He could hardly contain his disappointment. The old chest had never belonged to Gran at all, and their so-called treasure was nothing but a pile of ragged old cloths!

'I think we should forget all about the treasure now,' Anita said firmly as she and Vikram went to join their family and say goodbye to Rakesh and Esha. 'We're just going around in hopeless circles.'

'I know,' Vikram sighed. 'OK, Anita. No more treasure hunting.'

The twins were very subdued on the drive home. When they arrived back at the flat, Gran went straight to her room and Dad switched on the TV, while Vikram and Anita went to get a cold drink from the fridge.

'I'm just popping next door to see Shanti,' Mum told them. 'I'll only be a moment. Have you two finished your homework for Monday?'

'Yes, but we'd better practise those spellings again. Vikram – can you help me?' Anita asked.

Vikram nodded, and the twins sat down at the kitchen table where it was quiet.

'Spell *embarrassed*,' Vikram said, reading the word at the top of the spelling list. Then he began to laugh. 'We were pretty embarrassed today, weren't we, Anita? I thought we'd discovered the treasure – and it turned out to be a lot of old rags!'

'Never mind,' Anita grinned. She scribbled the word down. 'We did our best. But now I just don't think the treasure really exists. Let's not even bother thinking about it. What's the second spelling, Vik?'

Although Mum had said she'd only be a moment at Shanti's, she was actually gone for about half an hour. By the time she came back, Anita and Vikram had finished practising the spellings and they were making Dad a cup of tea.

'Sorry I was so long,' Mum said. 'Shanti just wouldn't stop talking! Anita, go and see if your gran would like some tea too.'

Anita sped down the hall to her gran's room and tapped gently on the door. No one answered, so Anita decided Gran must be having a nap. Quietly, she opened the door and peeped inside, just to check. But to Anita's surprise, Gran wasn't there. She went back along the hall, popping her head into every room, but Gran was nowhere to be found. Then, with a sinking feeling, Anita noticed that Gran's thick woollen shawl had gone from the hook by the front door where she had hung it when they came in.

'Mum! Dad! Vikram!' Anita was unable to keep her mounting worry out of her voice. 'Gran's disappeared!'

Chapter 7
Missing

'What do you mean – disappeared?' Mum cried.

'Gran's not in the flat,' Anita replied tearfully. 'And her shawl's gone.' She pointed to the empty hook.

'Has she taken her phone?' Dad asked.

'No, it's here on the hall table,' Vikram gestured towards it, his hand shaking.

'I'm going to look in the corridors, the lifts and the lobby.' Dad rushed to the front door.

'I'll come with you, Dad,' Vikram called, speeding after him.

'Anita, we'll go and ask all the neighbours if they've seen her anywhere,' Mum said, her face pale and anxious as she rushed out of the flat.

'Shanti, Gran's disappeared!' Anita blurted out helplessly when their neighbour opened her front door. 'We don't know where she's gone!'

'Oh no!' Shanti exclaimed. 'We need to organize a search party. Let's get the neighbours together.'

By the time Dad and Vikram came back upstairs, the corridor was crowded with neighbours offering support and assistance.

'Any luck?' Mum asked.

Dad shook his head. 'We've been up and down in the lift and spoken to people on all the floors but no one's seen her.' He suddenly looked very serious. 'I think she must have gone outside.'

Anita felt dread clutch at her heart. Where could Gran be? Of course, she used to go out by herself all the time, but it was different now that she was ill.

What if Gran forgot her name or where she lived? How would she ever make it home again? What if she tried to cross the road and got knocked down or something?

'Dad, we've got to find her!' Vikram said urgently.

'I think we should split up into groups and go out to look for her,' Shanti suggested, and all the neighbours murmured in agreement.

Quickly they organized themselves into small groups, and Vikram and Anita decided they would go with Shanti.

'Don't worry, my dears,' Shanti comforted them as they took the lift downstairs. 'Your gran can't have got very far. I expect she'll be sitting in one of the cafes close by, having a cup of tea.'

Once downstairs, the groups of people went off in different directions to search for Gran. Shanti and the twins walked down the main street, peering anxiously into all the shops and cafes, but there was no trace of Gran anywhere.

As they turned the corner, Shanti spotted a street seller next to a taxi rank. He was selling sugar cane juice. He had a little machine on wheels that crushed the canes of sugar and extracted all the sweet juices.

'Hello,' Shanti said. 'We're looking for an elderly woman with grey hair, wearing a white sari. Have you seen her coming past?'

The street seller shrugged. 'There are lots of elderly women around here,' he replied, feeding long sugar canes into the machine.

'Please,' Anita begged. 'Try to remember. My gran is really short, and she is wearing a red shawl over her sari. And she is wearing gold earrings with red stones.'

'Oh, yes,' the street seller said thoughtfully. 'I think I did see her. It must have been about twenty minutes ago.'

'Did you notice which way she went?' Vikram asked.

'She got into one of the taxis.' The street seller gestured in the direction of the taxi rank.

The twins glanced at each other in dismay. 'Are you sure?' Anita pleaded.

'Yes, I'm certain,' the street seller replied. 'I heard her ask the taxi driver to take her to the big white house next to the tourist market.'

'What?' Vikram was totally confused. 'That's where the famous artist lives, isn't it, Anita? That's what the sand sculptor said. Why on earth would Gran go there?'

For a moment, Anita looked as confused as her brother. Then suddenly, to Vikram's amazement, she groaned loudly and slapped her forehead. 'That's it!' she exclaimed. 'Why didn't I realize before?'

Vikram looked puzzled. 'Realize what?' he asked.

'You remember when we were at the beach and we set off in the car for the spice plantation?' The words were tumbling out of Anita's mouth so fast that they were almost incomprehensible. 'Gran said, "The treasure is there." But I don't think she meant the spice plantation at all!'

'So where did she mean?' Vikram began. Then he gasped. 'You think she meant the big white house?'

Anita nodded. 'Gran was looking out of the car window at the house when she said it, only I didn't realize that was the place she meant,' she explained. 'I think Gran's gone there.'

'Right, I'll fetch my car from the garage and we'll get over to this house right away,' Shanti said in a determined voice. 'One of you text your parents and tell them what's happening.'

Just a few minutes later, Shanti was driving the familiar route back to the beach where the tourist market was held. Anita sat in the front seat and texted her dad while Vikram fidgeted around in the back. For the first time in a while, he wasn't thinking about the treasure. He was too worried about Gran to have space in his head for anything else.

At last they reached the quiet street alongside the beach where the house was situated. Shanti drew the car to a halt and parked just outside the tall iron gates. As they piled out of the car, Anita stared up at the beautiful house. It looked even bigger and more impressive close-up, she thought. The ornately carved stone of the entrance gleamed brilliant white in the late afternoon sunshine. Through the gates Anita caught just a glimpse of the garden at the back of the house.

Could Gran really have come here? Anita pondered doubtfully. She was beginning to think she'd made a mistake …

'Hello there!' called a cheery voice.

The twins turned and saw the sand sculptor they'd met earlier that day coming towards them. He was carrying bags of shopping.

'Oh, hello,' Vikram replied. 'Have you finished making your sand sculptures for today?'

The young man nodded. 'Yes, and now the tide will come in and wash them away,' he smiled.

'That's sad!' Anita exclaimed. 'We saw them today, Auntie,' she told Shanti. 'They were so pretty.'

'It doesn't matter.' The young man shrugged. 'I'll make some more tomorrow. There's always plenty of sand!' He nodded at the house. 'So is this your man who makes elephants? I saw your gran here not long ago.'

'Our gran?' Anita repeated.

'Yes, I was on my way to the shops and I saw her ringing the bell on the gate,' the man told them. Then, with a friendly wave, he walked on.

'Gran is here!' Anita gasped, overjoyed.

'Quick, let's ring the bell,' Vikram urged Shanti.

The bell was attached to an intercom and when the green light came on, a woman's voice said, 'Hello, this is the housekeeper. How may I help you?'

'Hello?' Anita said breathlessly into the intercom. 'Hello, we think our gran's in your house and we'd like to come in and bring her home, please.'

'And who are you?' the voice asked suspiciously.

'Here, let me talk to her.' Shanti moved forward to the intercom. 'Look, sorry, but we're in rather a hurry,' she told the housekeeper. 'We're looking for a missing person and we think she might be here. Please can you let us in?'

'The master of the house is busy, and he's asked me not to disturb him,' the housekeeper replied. 'I can't possibly let you in unless he says so.'

Shanti frowned. 'But this is an emergency!'

'The housekeeper's not going to let us in,' Vikram said to Anita as Shanti continued to argue with the voice on the intercom. 'What are we going to do?'

'I don't know yet,' Anita replied, her face determined. 'But we're not leaving without Gran!'

Chapter 8
The Man Who Makes Elephants

'Look, we think you have a missing person inside this house, and we're not going to move until you let us in.' Shanti was still talking with the housekeeper. The twins could see that her usually cheerful face was red and flustered. 'Or shall we call the police?'

'You can call the police if you like, but I won't let them in either,' the housekeeper replied firmly. 'The master of the house told me he wasn't expecting any visitors and I wasn't to disturb him under any circumstances, so I cannot let you in. And anyway, I have no idea who you are. You might be newspaper reporters, and this could just be a trick to get inside.'

'Well, really!' Shanti's voice was full of outrage. She wasn't prepared to let the housekeeper get away with that! As she resumed the argument, Vikram and Anita walked a little way alongside the wall, trying to find a way to see into the garden.

'I can hear voices on the other side of the wall,' Anita said suddenly, coming to a stop. 'There's someone in the garden, Vikram!'

'Is it Gran?' Vikram asked. The twins stood still and listened hard, but it was impossible to make out who was speaking. They could definitely hear voices though, and also the tinkle of teacups against saucers.

'We need to look over this wall!' Anita said firmly. 'Find me something to stand on, Vikram.'

Vikram looked up and down the street. Then he spotted a large, sturdy plastic crate that a delivery van must have deposited on the pavement outside a nearby shop. He grabbed it quickly and took it back to Anita.

'This looks pretty strong,' Vikram said, turning the crate upside down and sliding it up against the wall.

Anita was about to hop up on to the crate when Vikram stopped her. 'How come you're the one getting to look over the wall?' he demanded. 'I want to do it!'

'Because I'm the tallest,' Anita retorted. Vikram couldn't argue with that. Anita was taller than him, although only by a centimetre or two. So he waited impatiently as Anita climbed on to the crate and grasped the top of the wall with both hands. Now she was just tall enough to peer over it.

Anita looked around eagerly. A beautiful landscaped garden was laid out in front of her, with emerald-green lawns, tall trees, a marble fountain and borders swelling with the vibrant colours of flowers in full bloom. Dotted here and there throughout the garden were wonderful sculptures of elephants carved in white marble.

'Elephants!' Anita murmured to herself. 'And, thank goodness, there's Gran!'

Anita had spotted a wicker table and chairs laid out under the shade of the trees. Her gran sat in one of the chairs, sipping tea. She looked fine, Anita thought, overcome with relief. In the other chair was a man Anita had never seen before. He had black hair flecked with grey and a black beard, and he wore comfortable old clothes that were ripped and stained with paint.

'What can you see, Anita?' Vikram called urgently. Just a short distance away, Shanti was still talking into the intercom and hadn't noticed what they were up to. 'Can you see Gran?'

'Yes, and I can see lots of elephants, and the man who made them!' Anita replied. 'He's having tea with Gran.'

'Let me see!' Vikram urged, trying to climb up on to the crate alongside Anita. But there was only room for one of them, so, looking a bit annoyed, he had to get down again.

'What should we do now?' Anita asked, glancing over at Shanti. Their neighbour still hadn't managed to persuade the housekeeper to open the gates.

'Try to get Gran's attention,' Vikram suggested.

Anita looked over the wall again and began waving her arms, hoping Gran would notice her. But Gran didn't even glance in her direction.

'It's not working,' Anita said to Vikram.

'You'll have to shout then,' Vikram replied. 'Go on, do it!'

Feeling very self-conscious, Anita shouted, 'GRAN!' as loudly as she could. 'GRAN!'

Gran looked around and the man instantly jumped up out of his chair.

'Who are you?' he called, striding angrily across the lawn towards them. 'What's your name and why are you shouting?'

'I'm Anita and that's my gran. She disappeared from our house and – '

The man turned to Gran, who had struggled up out of her chair and was coming towards them. 'Is this really your granddaughter?' he asked gently, his frown melting away. 'Do you know her?'

Gran looked a little puzzled. 'Of course I know her, Dev,' she said. 'It's Rajni.'

'Rajni!' the man repeated.

'That's my mum,' Anita said quickly. 'My gran mixes our names up sometimes. Please, you have to believe me!'

Meanwhile, Shanti had been defeated by the housekeeper, who'd sent her away, and she'd come over to Vikram.

'What's going on?' Shanti asked. 'Why was Anita shouting?'

'Gran's in the garden with the man who makes elephants and she's told him Anita's name is Rajni, so now the man who makes elephants doesn't believe that Anita is really Gran's granddaughter,' Vikram gabbled in one long breath.

'Goodness me!' Shanti gasped.

Anita was still trying to convince the man called Dev that she knew Gran. 'Look, I have photos of me and my twin brother Vikram with our gran,' she said, taking her phone out of her pocket. 'You can see for yourself. But your housekeeper won't let us in.'

'I think you'd better go around to the main gates and I'll let you in myself,' Dev said, looking rather bewildered. 'Then we can sort this out once and for all.'

'All right,' Anita agreed. As she steadied herself, ready to climb down from the box, she was glad to see that Dev took Gran's arm and very kindly helped her back across the grass to her seat. Whoever the man was, he really seemed to care about Gran.

'The man's going to let us in,' Anita told Shanti and Vikram. 'His name's Dev.'

'Is Gran OK?' Vikram asked anxiously. 'I'd better text Mum and Dad right away and tell them she's been found.'

Anita nodded. 'Yes, Gran's fine,' she replied. 'Dev's being very nice to her.'

'I wonder how your gran knows him?' Shanti said. 'I've heard he's very rich and famous.'

The ornate iron gates slowly swung open as they approached. Then Dev appeared through the front door of the house, closing it behind him with a soft click. To Anita's relief, he didn't look annoyed any more.

'Welcome,' Dev said with a smile. 'I must apologize for my housekeeper. We are plagued with newspaper reporters and photographers ringing the doorbell all day long. She was trying to protect me.'

'Look, that lady, Meera Sharma, really is our gran,' Anita said earnestly. Quickly she scrolled through the picture gallery on her phone and showed Dev some photos of the family with Gran.

'I see.' Dev looked rather concerned. 'Does your gran get things mixed up quite a bit?'

'Sometimes,' Anita replied sadly. 'She's not well.'

'Look, we know you're really famous, and we're sorry to disturb you,' Vikram told Dev. 'But you see, we lost our gran, and we've been trying to find the family treasure, and Gran said it was here so we guessed she must have come to your house ... '

Dev's face betrayed his confusion. 'I think you'd better tell me the whole story, right from the beginning,' he said.

Chapter 9
At Last!

Dev led the twins and Shanti around the side of the house and into the garden. The garden looked even more spectacular than Anita had first thought. There were sea views from the terrace, and some of the marble elephant statues were hidden among the shrubbery with just their trunks poking out among the leaves. It was a grand and glorious garden, but it was also a fun one. Anita especially liked a sculpture of three baby elephants holding on to each other's tails.

When they reached the chairs under the trees, Anita saw that Gran had fallen asleep and her shawl had slipped off on to the grass. She sat down in the seat next to her, picked up the shawl and covered Gran with it.

'Now then, start from the beginning and tell me everything,' Dev said, settling himself back in his chair.

So, taking turns, Vikram and Anita explained how Gran had told them about the family treasure and about 'the man who makes elephants'. They told how they'd tried to find him at the market, and then how they'd thought it might be the sand sculptor. Looking a bit embarrassed, the twins even explained how they'd looked around Rakesh and Esha's spice plantation and ended up finding a chest full of old rags, which made Dev and Shanti laugh.

'Then we realized that Gran meant the treasure was right here, in this house,' Vikram finished up. 'That's why Gran's here now – and that's how we guessed where to find her.' He stared hopefully at Dev. 'Do you have the treasure?'

To the twins' intense dismay, Dev shook his head. 'I'm pretty sure there's no treasure belonging to your gran here,' he said. 'I don't know why she would think that.'

'So how do you know Meera?' Shanti asked curiously.

Dev smiled. 'She was my nanny when I was a little boy. This house is my family home. Your grandad was our driver. He took my father to work in the city every day. And your gran looked after me.'

'That must have been a really long time ago!' Vikram said, staring at the flecks of grey in the man's hair. Then he blushed as Anita and Shanti both laughed. Luckily, Dev laughed too.

'It was many years ago,' he said, staring off into the distance as if he was reliving old memories. 'I loved your gran. She was great fun, and she taught me how to play cricket.'

'Us too!' Anita told him.

'But then, when I was seven, my parents decided to send me to school in England,' Dev said. 'I was sent to live with relatives in London and I remember how lonely and miserable I felt when I had to say goodbye to your gran and grandad.' He sighed. 'They left very soon after that and went to work for another family. I hadn't seen your gran since then, until she turned up today. I was working on my latest project and I didn't want to be disturbed, but I was delighted to see her.'

'Do you think Gran and Grandad might have left the treasure here when they changed jobs?' Vikram asked.

Anita frowned. 'That doesn't make sense. Why would they need new jobs if they had loads of treasure? They could have lived like a king and queen if they had gold and jewels!'

'Sorry, but I really don't think there is any treasure,' Dev said with a shrug.

'Oh yes, there is!' a sleepy voice interrupted.

Vikram, Anita, Shanti and Dev all sat up and stared at Gran, who yawned a little and then nodded her head. 'Your grandad and I left a big wooden chest in one of the outhouses on the other side of the garden,' Gran explained. 'We couldn't take all the family treasure with us when we changed jobs, so we left some of it here. We were always going to come back for it, but I think we just got so busy, we forgot ... ' Her voice tailed away.

Vikram looked at Dev. 'So is the chest still here?' he asked, trembling with excitement.

'Well, I don't know.' Dev frowned. 'There are four or five outhouses stuffed with junk that belonged to my parents. I only came back to India from America a few months ago and I haven't got around to clearing them out yet.'

'Could we go and look?' Anita begged Dev, as Vikram's phone buzzed.

'Of course.' Dev got out of his chair and helped Gran to her feet. 'I want to find this treasure as much as you do!'

'Our mum and dad have just texted that they're outside,' said Vikram. 'Can they come too?'

'Certainly,' Dev replied. 'I'll go and let them in.' And a few moments later, he returned with the twins' parents, who were both looking rather bewildered.

'What's going on?' Dad asked. 'What was that strange text you sent us about Gran coming here to look for her treasure, Vikram?'

'The treasure's here, Dad, it really is!' Vikram assured him. 'Anita and I have been looking for it all day in different places, but Gran says it's here.'

'It is!' Gran said firmly.

'But Mum, you don't have any treasure,' the twins' mother told Gran, shaking her head.

'Shall we go and find out?' Dev suggested. 'Follow me, everyone!'

Dev led the way across the lawns and around the other side of the house. There was a large courtyard with two big garages filled with impressively glossy sports cars that made the children's eyes light up. Next to the garages were stables, and Anita would have loved to stop to pat the horses, but Dev took them behind the stables to reveal another row of warehouse-type buildings.

'That's my workroom,' Dev said, pointing at one of them. The door stood open and the twins peeped in. They were fascinated to see paintings of elephants propped up around the walls. An unfinished painting stood on an easel and there were lumps of marble here and there, waiting to be carved. The floor of the workroom was spattered with a profusion of multicoloured paint stains and white chips of marble.

'That one.' Gran stopped and pointed at the third building in the row. 'That's where we left the treasure chest.'

'OK, let's have a look, then.' Dev took some keys from his pocket and opened the door. Anita and Vikram waited in silence, tense with excitement.

Sunlight flooded into the building, lighting up every dusty corner. It was full of rickety old furniture like Rakesh and Esha's old warehouses. There were also crates of books and bags of clothes piled on top of each other, as well as some of Dev's old marble statues that were chipped and cracked.

'We'll never find anything in here,' Vikram said. But Gran was already pointing confidently at a solid-looking wooden chest near the back of the room, half-concealed under a pair of heavy velvet curtains.

'That's it!' Gran said.

89

Chapter 10
The Real Treasure

Dev and Dad grabbed the chest and hauled it out from the rest of the junk.

'It's locked,' Dad said, trying the catch.

'Try this!' And Vikram produced the key from his pocket like a magician pulling a rabbit out of a hat. His parents stared at him, astounded.

'Gran gave it to me,' Vikram explained. He and Anita watched intently, their hearts racing with excitement, as Dad turned the key and the chest clicked open.

The lid was so heavy, Dad and Dev struggled to lift it. When they finally did, Vikram and Anita couldn't help gasping with disappointment. Inside the chest were piles of scribbled handwritten notes, old postcards, a couple of dolls with missing arms and legs, a very scratched and worn cricket bat and some old-fashioned board games.

'This isn't treasure!' Vikram whispered to Anita. But Gran had knelt down in front of the chest and was excavating it, pulling items out and examining them closely as she beamed with delight.

'This is the cricket bat my brother gave me for my birthday,' she said, handing it up to Vikram. 'You and Anita can have it now.' The twins glanced at each other in surprise as they realized Gran recognized everything in the chest. 'And these are my dolls and games from when I was little,' Gran added as she sat the dolls on the floor. 'This one is called Rita and that one is called Manju.'

'Mum, what are these?' the twins' mother asked, scooping up a handful of the papers and studying them one by one. 'Oh, they're recipes!' she exclaimed. 'You wrote these down yourself?'

Gran nodded proudly. 'I used to invent all my own recipes,' she explained. 'And look, my brothers sent me these postcards when they moved away. Chandan joined the army, Suraj moved to America with his wife and Hitesh went to live in Mumbai. I saved every letter and postcard they ever sent me. They're all here.'

Vikram and Anita gazed at Gran in astonishment. They hadn't heard her speak so clearly and so confidently, without getting muddled, for months.

Gran was burrowing further into the chest, and she had a story to tell about everything she took out. There were photos of her with her brothers when she was very small, bundles of letters, more postcards, books and also some very old vinyl records of music from Bollywood films.

'Your grandad and I loved these films,' Gran said wistfully, staring at the colourful covers in her hands. 'Oh, and look! This is your grandad's old watch.' She took a brass pocket watch from the chest and held it up. 'This belonged to your grandad's father, you know,' she told the twins. 'But it stopped working so your grandad bought a new one. We always meant to get this repaired, but we never got around to it.'

Despite their disappointment at the lack of gold and jewels, Vikram and Anita were soon won over by Gran's enthusiasm. They could hardly remember their grandad, so hearing stories about him was fascinating. As well as the watch, there were some photographs of him dressed in his driver's uniform, and there was also a medal and a certificate he'd been given for saving a child from drowning.

'I can just about remember him telling me all about that, although I was very young,' Mum said. 'I'd forgotten about it until now, though.'

'Yes,' said Gran. 'Grandad and I were out for a walk, and we saw a little girl fall into the river.

Grandad was very brave and dived in to rescue her. It was reported in the newspapers.' She picked up a bundle of yellowing newspaper clippings and handed them to the twins.

'Grandad was a hero,' Vikram exclaimed as they leafed through the clippings. He and Anita had never heard this story before. 'Cool!'

Right at the bottom of the chest was a red sari, heavily embroidered with gold thread.

'That's my wedding sari,' Gran said softly. She gathered the sari into her arms and pressed the silky material gently against her cheek.

'I think it's time we took this family treasure home where it belongs,' Dad said, and Vikram and Anita nodded.

The twins, Mum and Shanti helped Gran to repack the chest carefully. Then Dad and Dev picked up the chest and carried it out to the car. Bright-eyed and smiling, Gran followed them, leaning on Shanti's arm.

'Shanti told us that treasure isn't always gold and jewels,' Anita said to Mum and Vikram. 'And she was right! I haven't seen Gran so happy for ages. She was almost like she used to be.'

'She could remember so much about the past, as well,' Vikram marvelled. 'Even though yesterday she forgot how to switch the kettle on!'

'Gran's illness means that very often her memories of the past are a lot sharper and clearer than her life now,' Mum explained, sliding one arm around Anita and the other around Vikram as they walked through the garden to the car. 'You can help by talking to her about the old days, and about our family history.'

'We will,' Anita promised. 'It was so interesting to hear all that stuff about her brothers, and about Grandad being a hero. I never knew any of that.'

'Oh, I've got a really great idea!' Vikram said suddenly.

'Modest, aren't you?' Anita teased.

Vikram poked his tongue out at her. 'We could take photos of everything in the chest and make a slideshow on our tablets,' he suggested. 'Then we can look at all the letters and other stuff with

Gran whenever she likes. She must have loads more stories to tell us.'

'We could take the photos into school to show Miss Pinto and our class too,' Anita suggested.

'I think that's a really good idea,' Mum declared. 'And it might be the best thing anyway – just in case Gran puts the things away and forgets where they are.'

The twins both nodded eagerly. They had reached the gates by now; Shanti was in her car, about to leave, and Dad and Gran were in the other car waiting for them.

'Thank you very much,' Anita said to Dev, 'for being so kind to Gran and helping us find all that special treasure.'

'You're not sorry it wasn't gold and jewels?' Dev asked, his eyes twinkling.

'Nope!' Vikram replied firmly. 'Because Anita and I think that our family is the greatest treasure of all.'